ITSE SELU
Cherokee Harvest Festival

by Daniel Pennington
illustrated by Don Stewart

 Charlesbridge

The editor is indebted to the following for their contribution to this book.
Each person has generously shared her or his love and knowledge of Cherokee
history and culture in order to assist us in our effort to achieve authenticity and
accuracy in our text and illustrations. *Wado!*

Jeff Briley, Curator of Collections, Oklahoma Historical Society; Carter Blue Clark,
Executive Vice President, Oklahoma City University; Carol Dunn, Cherokee
National Historical Society; Joan Greene, Archivist, Museum of the Cherokee;
Geneva (Mama Gene) Jackson; Dillard Jordan, Historical Property Manager,
Sequoyah Home Site; Marie Junaluska, Indian Clerk, Eastern Band of the
Cherokee; John Ketcher, Deputy Principal Chief of the Cherokee Nation;
Duane King, Assistant Director, Smithsonian Institution National Museum of the
American Indian; Chester Kowen, Photo Archivist, Oklahoma Historical Society;
John Lovett, Librarian, Western History Collections, University of Oklahoma;
David Moore, Archaeologist, North Carolina Dept. of Cultural Resources;
Prentice Robinson, Education Director, Education Center of the Cherokee Nation.

Note: We have elected to employ vocabulary from the eastern dialect
of the Cherokee language since our story is placed in the original
Cherokee homeland, the southeastern section of the United States.

Published by
Charlesbridge Publishing
85 Main Street, Watertown, MA 02172 • (617) 926-0329

Printed in the United States of America
(sc) 10 9 8 7 6 5 4 3 2
(hc) 10 9 8 7 6 5 4 3 2

Printed on Recycled Paper

Library of Congress Cataloging-in-Publication Data
Pennington, Daniel, 1961–
  Itse selu: Cherokee harvest festival / by Daniel Pennington; illustrated by Don Stewart.
    p.   cm.
  ISBN 0-88106-850-0 (softcover)
  ISBN 0-88106-851-9 (reinforced for library use)
  1. Cherokee Indians—Rites and ceremonies—Juvenile literature. 2. Cherokee
Indians—Social life and customs—Juvenile literature. 3. Harvest festivals—Southern
States—Juvenile literature. [1. Cherokee Indians. 2. Indians of North America.
3. Harvest festivals.] I. Stewart, Don, 1961– ill. II. Title.
E99.C85P46 1994
394.2'64'089975—dc20   93-27147
                                                                          CIP
                                                                           AC

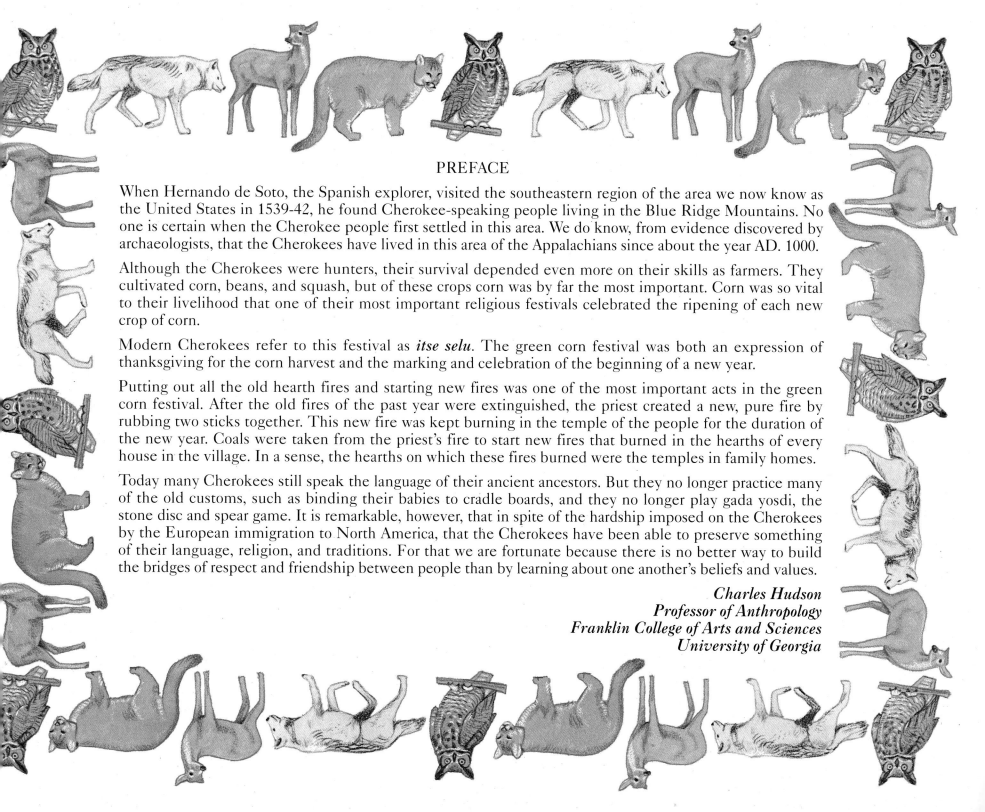

PREFACE

When Hernando de Soto, the Spanish explorer, visited the southeastern region of the area we now know as the United States in 1539-42, he found Cherokee-speaking people living in the Blue Ridge Mountains. No one is certain when the Cherokee people first settled in this area. We do know, from evidence discovered by archaeologists, that the Cherokees have lived in this area of the Appalachians since about the year AD. 1000.

Although the Cherokees were hunters, their survival depended even more on their skills as farmers. They cultivated corn, beans, and squash, but of these crops corn was by far the most important. Corn was so vital to their livelihood that one of their most important religious festivals celebrated the ripening of each new crop of corn.

Modern Cherokees refer to this festival as *itse selu*. The green corn festival was both an expression of thanksgiving for the corn harvest and the marking and celebration of the beginning of a new year.

Putting out all the old hearth fires and starting new fires was one of the most important acts in the green corn festival. After the old fires of the past year were extinguished, the priest created a new, pure fire by rubbing two sticks together. This new fire was kept burning in the temple of the people for the duration of the new year. Coals were taken from the priest's fire to start new fires that burned in the hearths of every house in the village. In a sense, the hearths on which these fires burned were the temples in family homes.

Today many Cherokees still speak the language of their ancient ancestors. But they no longer practice many of the old customs, such as binding their babies to cradle boards, and they no longer play gada yosdi, the stone disc and spear game. It is remarkable, however, that in spite of the hardship imposed on the Cherokees by the European immigration to North America, that the Cherokees have been able to preserve something of their language, religion, and traditions. For that we are fortunate because there is no better way to build the bridges of respect and friendship between people than by learning about one another's beliefs and values.

Charles Hudson
Professor of Anthropology
Franklin College of Arts and Sciences
University of Georgia

Little Wolf blinked as he looked out at the bright, September morning. The village bustled with activity.

"Tonight is the feast!" he remembered excitedly. He saw Mother cooking by the fire.

Starting late this afternoon, the entire village would gather to celebrate another day of **Itse Selu**, the Green Corn Festival.

The celebration lasted four days. Each year, just when the first ears of corn turned sweet and yellow, the great festival was held. Itse Selu was a feast of thanksgiving, and it marked the beginning of the new year.

Itse Selu *(it say shay LOO´)* Newly ripened corn, known as green corn.

Throughout the village everyone was hard at work.

Little Wolf's sister, Skye, finished eating her breakfast of beans and **selu**. Mother made the hominy from "old corn," corn harvested last year. It was *forbidden* to harvest or eat this year's corn before Itse Selu.

"Little Wolf, where are you? You're not going to sleep through Itse Selu, are you?" teased Skye as she walked toward the river with her empty clay water pot.

selu *(shay LOO')* corn

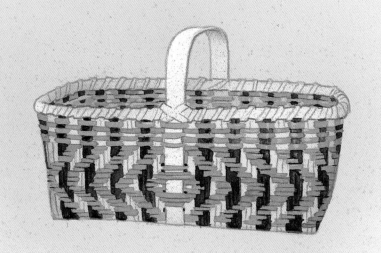

In the morning, everyone in the village bathed before starting their day. On his way to bathe in the river, Little Wolf stopped and peeked into Mother's cooking pot.

"Is this for the feast tonight?" Little Wolf asked. The food smelled so good. It made his stomach growl.

"Yes, and I will cook two of your favorites as soon as Father brings back the fish and turkey," answered Mother. "If you are hungry, Little Wolf, have some selu and **tuya**, but take your bath first!"

tuya *(TOO´yah)* beans

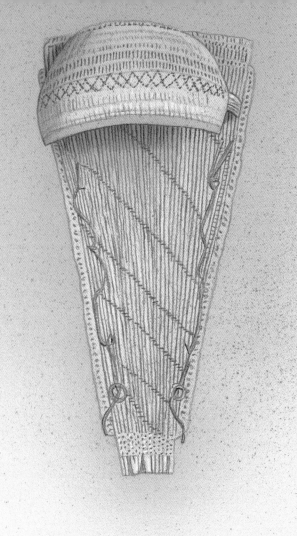

Little Wolf stopped to tickle his sister's chin. "Are you ready for the festival, Sutega?" Sutega cooed and smiled at Little Wolf from her cradleboard.

Mother carried Sutega on her back, in the cradleboard. Sometimes she leaned the cradleboard against their house or under a shady tree.

Because the cradleboard was always close by, Mother was able to keep watch over her **usdi** and still get her work done.

usdi *(oos DIH´)* baby

Little Wolf gobbled down his breakfast and then ran over to see Grandmother. She was making a pair of **dilasulo** for him. The dilasulo were made of soft deerskin.

"Grandmother, are you sure they will be finished by this afternoon?" asked Little Wolf.

Grandmother gently smiled and said, "Just as I promised you, Little Wolf! Today you will wear your new dilasulo. Don't worry!"

dilasulo *(DIH´ lah su lo)* footwear

Returning with the fresh **ama,** Skye happily sang out to her brother, "Hello, sleepyhead!"

Skye was a big help to her family. She worked in the garden and went to the forest to gather berries and nuts. She sewed deerskin clothes. Her favorite work, though, was making clay pottery. Everyone in the village wanted one of Skye's beautiful pots.

"See you later, Skye," called Little Wolf as he ran off to find his friend.

ama *(ah MAH´)* water

In the forest, Little Wolf found Little Buffalo, his best friend, throwing a wooden spear.

The **anisgaya** patiently taught the boys to hunt and fish. "You cannot be skillful hunters and fishermen until you know exactly how the animals live," they explained. So the boys learned to carefully observe the ways of the animals.

One day the boys studied a spider spinning its web. This helped the boys learn to weave webbed fish nets. Soon they would begin taking net-making lessons from Water Spider, one of the anisgaya. No one else in the whole tribe could make nets as skillfully as Water Spider.

anisgaya *(ah NEES' gah yah)* men

Little Buffalo and Little Wolf hid in the underbrush. "Look!" whispered Little Buffalo. "**Ahwi!**" In silence, they watched the deer until it bounded away.

"I wish we were old enough to hunt," sighed Little Wolf. "What a prize that deer would have been for Itse Selu."

When the boys became real hunters, they would use spears, bows and arrows, and blowguns. A blowgun was a hollow cane from which a sharp dart was blown. Powerful lungs were required to project the dart.

It took much practice and hard work to become a great hunter.

ahwi *(ah WIH´)* deer

"Get your **gada yosdi** stick," Little Wolf called to Little Buffalo.

Little Buffalo laughed. "Do you want to lose again?"

"Not a chance!" boasted Little Wolf. "I've been practicing with my uncle, so be prepared." Gada yosdi was a favorite game played by the boys. It helped them improve their throwing skills.

Little Wolf won twice before it was time to race home for Itse Selu.

gada yosdi *(gah DAH´ yo sdee)*
An ancient game played by
Cherokee. Each player threw
a bamboo stick at a rolling
stone. The object of the
game was to throw to
the spot where the
player estimated the
stone would stop rolling.

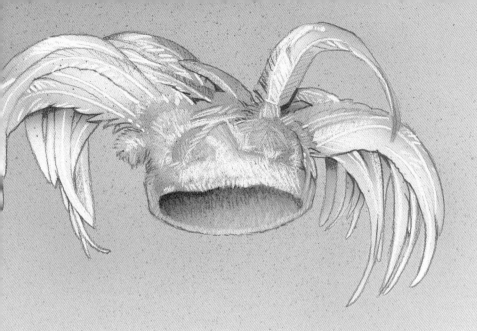

The late afternoon sun signaled the time for everyone in the village to gather for the feast and celebration. Before they left their homes, they swept the houses clean and put out all the fires. Each family took some of their freshly picked corn to the feast.

"I hope everyone will notice my new moccasins!" thought Little Wolf who was intently watching his feet as he walked.

The people sat down outside the council house. Inside, the priest lit the new **gotvdi** that symbolized the new year. Then he said a prayer to the Great Creator.

"Thank you for a year of good harvest and hunting. We hope the new year will again provide us with food. We must forget any quarrels that we have between us so that we may start the new year together, with a happy spirit. Let the feast begin!"

gotvdi *(go tuh VIH´)* fire

After eating lots of food at the harvest feast, everyone began to relax. The light of the blazing sunset glowed in the western sky. Sundown announced that it was time for the next set of dances to begin. The dancers performed until sunrise.

It was dark when the sundown dances finished. And it was finally time for Skye's favorite part of Itse Selu — story time. Her grandfather was one of the village storytellers. Eagerly she asked, "Grandfather, what story will you tell us tonight?"

"Tonight you will hear about **tsistu**, the clever rabbit, and **tlvdatsi**, the foolish wildcat," answered Grandfather with twinkling eyes.

tsistu *(jees DOO ́)* rabbit
tlvdatsi *(tluh dah TSIH ́)* mountain lion

One fine summer day, Rabbit found Wildcat digging a well. Rabbit refused to help dig, so Wildcat told him, "When I find water, you may not have any of it."

After the well was dug, Rabbit came by and stole some water. This made Wildcat angry so he decided to punish Rabbit. He made a doll and covered it with a sticky gum-glue and called it Stickyman. Then he set Stickyman near the well and hid.

That night, when he came to the well, Rabbit saw Stickyman. "Who are you?" Rabbit asked. Stickyman, of course, made no reply. Rabbit became impatient. So impatient that he hit Stickyman. His hand stuck tight! He could not get it loose! As Rabbit struggled to get free, Wildcat jumped on him.

"Now what should I do with you, Rabbit? Throw you in the lake?" shouted Wildcat. Rabbit told Wildcat how much he loved to swim in the lake, so Wildcat made another plan. "I will tie you to the apple tree, Rabbit," declared Wildcat. Rabbit said, "Yes, please! Apples are a favorite of mine." Wildcat frowned and changed his mind again.

Then Rabbit said, "Do anything you like, but please do not throw me in the raspberry patch!" Instantly Wildcat unstuck Rabbit from Stickyman and threw Rabbit right into the berry patch.

"Ha! Ha! I tricked you, silly Wildcat," jeered the clever rabbit as he raced away in freedom to his home hidden under the berry brambles.

Skye and Little Wolf were asleep soon after Grandfather finished his story. Mother stayed awake through the night talking with her neighbors.

When the eastern horizon began to turn pale gray, Mother gently called, "Skye, Little Wolf, please wake up. The Green Corn Dance will soon begin." Sleepily, the children sat up. The drumming and singing began.

The slow solemn corn dance began. One of the **anigehya** dancers wore tortoise-shell rattles on her ankles that went claddle-claddle, claddle-claddle as she stepped in rhythm to the drum. The sacred dance was a prayer of thanksgiving for this year's corn. The dance was timed to end just as the sun rose. Sunrise symbolized springtime, the season when next year's corn would be planted. Little Wolf and Skye hardly breathed as the powerful mood of the dance enfolded them.

anigehya *(ah nee gay YAH´)* women

When the Green Corn Dance ended it was time to go home. The family walked home in the quiet beauty of dawn. **Utsi** carried a glowing coal, from the New Year fire, in a special clay pot. She would use it to start the family's new year fire. It was her duty to keep the fire burning for a whole year. The fire could not be extinguished until next year's Itse Selu celebration.

Skye and Little Wolf were asleep almost before they snuggled under their blankets. "Skye," sighed Little Wolf, "someday I hope I will be as clever as tsistu the rabbit!"

Utsi, the last to fall asleep, smiled and whispered, "Sweet dreams, my children. Happy New Year."

utsi *(ooh TSEE´)* mother

Sequoyah (1770?-1843) was a Cherokee Indian who is remembered as being the only individual to ever single-handedly devise a written language. Before Sequoyah, the Cherokee language existed only in the form of the spoken word. During his service in the U.S. Army, Sequoyah was exposed to the idea of language as something that could be represented as marks on paper. This amazed Sequoyah. He wanted to be able to write in his own language. After years of hard work he invented an alphabet, called a syllabary, where each syllable-sound in the Cherokee dialect was represented by one symbol. There were 86 signs in Sequoyah's syllabary. By learning these 86 shapes anyone could read or write any word in the Cherokee language. Sequoyah's syllabary helped unite the Cherokee nation. They were able to start a newspaper and print books and magazines. The tallest tree in the world, the Sequoia, is named for the Cherokee who was a giant among his people.

Cherokee Syllabary

a		e	i	o	u	v
D a		R e	T i	Ꮼ o	Ᏺ u	i v
Ꮝ ga Ꮖ ka		Ꮊ ge	Ꮿ gi	A go	J gu	Ꭼ gv
Ꮒ ha		Ꮻ he	Ꮩ hi	F ho	Ꮐ hu	Ꭴ hv
Ꮃ la		Ꮨ le	Ꮅ li	Ꮪ lo	M lu	Ꮑ lv
Ꮉ ma		Ꮍ me	Ꮇ mi	Ꮕ mo	Ꮹ mu	
Ꮧ na Ꮏ hna Ꮐ nah		Ꮄ ne	Ꮒ ni	Ꮓ no	Ꮔ nu	Ꮕ nv
Ꮖ qua		Ꮗ que	Ꮜ qui	Ꮙ quo	Ꮚ quu	Ꮝ quv
Ꮜ sa Ꮝ s		Ꮞ se	Ꮟ si	Ꮠ so	Ꮡ su	Ꮢ sv
Ꮣ da Ꮤ ta		Ꮥ de Ꮦ te	Ꮧ di Ꮨ ti	Ꮩ do	Ꮪ du	Ꮫ dv
Ꮬ dla Ꮭ tla		Ꮮ tle	Ꮯ tli	Ꮰ tlo	Ꮲ tlu	Ꮳ tlv
Ꮳ tsa		Ꮴ tse	Ꮵ tsi	Ꮶ tso	Ꮷ tsu	Ꮸ tsv
Ꮹ wa		Ꮺ we	Ꮻ wi	Ꮼ wo	Ꮽ wu	Ꮾ wv
Ꮿ ya		Ᏸ ye	Ᏹ yi	Ᏺ yo	Ᏻ yu	Ᏼ yv

Sounds Represented by Vowels	
a, as <u>a</u> in <u>father</u>, or short as <u>a</u> in <u>rival</u>	o, as <u>o</u> in <u>note</u>, approaching <u>aw</u> in <u>law</u>
e, as <u>a</u> in <u>hate</u>, or short as <u>e</u> in <u>met</u>	u, as <u>oo</u> in <u>fool</u>, or short as <u>u</u> in <u>pull</u>
i, as <u>i</u> in long <u>e</u> in peek, or short as <u>i</u> in <u>pit</u>	v, as <u>u</u> in <u>but</u>, nasalize